BAD  KITTY
for
PRESIDENT

NICK BRUEL

SQUARE
FISH

ROARING BROOK PRESS
New York

To Rosa
and her family

SQUARE
FISH

An Imprint of Macmillan
175 Fifth Avenue
New York, NY 10010
mackids.com

Square Fish and the Square Fish logo are trademarks of Macmillan and
are used by Roaring Brook Press under license from Macmillan.

Our books may be purchased in bulk for promotional, educational, or business use. Please
contact your local bookseller or the Macmillan Corporate and Premium Sales Department at
(800) 221-7945 ext. 5442 or by e-mail at MacmillanSpecialMarkets@macmillan.com.

Library of Congress Cataloging-in-Publication Data
Bruel, Nick.
Bad Kitty for president / Nick Bruel.
   p. cm.
"A Neal Porter Book."
Summary: Kitty decides to run for President of the Neighborhood Cat Club.
ISBN 978-1-250-07962-6 (paperback)
[1. Politics, Practical—Fiction. 2. Elections—Fiction. 3. Cats—Fiction.]
I. Title.
   PZ7.B82832Baf 2012
[E]—dc23

2011018401

Originally published in the United States by Roaring Brook Press
First Square Fish Edition: 2012
Square Fish Reissue Edition: 2016
Square Fish logo designed by Filomena Tuosto

1 3 5 7 9 10 8 6 4 2

AR: 4.5 / LEXILE: 690L

• CONTENTS •

INTRODUCTION
OLD KITTY 5

CHAPTER ONE
THE PRIMARIES 13

CHAPTER TWO
THE ENDORSEMENT 37

CHAPTER THREE
ON THE CAMPAIGN TRAIL 53

CHAPTER FOUR
MEDIA AND MONEY 66

CHAPTER FIVE
THE DEBATE 91

CHAPTER SIX
ELECTION DAY! 106

CHAPTER SEVEN
THE RESULTS 115

APPENDIX ONE 136

APPENDIX TWO 142

As you read this book, you'll notice
that there is a ★ following some of the words.

These words are defined
in the Glossary at the back of this book.

•INTRODUCTION•
OLD KITTY

This is Old Kitty.

Old Kitty can't hear very well anymore. Old Kitty's eyes don't work so well anymore. Old Kitty's claws aren't as sharp as they used to be, and his bones sometimes creak when he walks.

Old Kitty happens to be the president★ of the Neighborhood Cat Club. But not for long.

Next week, Old Kitty will leave office★ and give up his role as the president of the Neighborhood Cat Club. Why? It's not just because he's old and tired. It's also because he will have served two full terms in office, which is the longest any kitty is allowed to be president of the Neighborhood Cat Club.

But Old Kitty won't mind leaving office. At four years a term . . .

that's eight whole years Old Kitty has been president . . .

and eight years is about half of a cat's natural lifetime.

But Old Kitty will leave office knowing that he did the best job he could. Being president is a very, very hard job. Being president means often working late into the night and living with the constant stress of having so much responsibility. In many ways, being president is the most difficult job there is, and Old Kitty has been pretty worn out by it.

8 YEARS AGO

6 YEARS AGO

But don't feel too bad about Old Kitty. He still has many good years ahead of him. After all . . .

4 YEARS AGO

2 YEARS AGO

11

Old Kitty is only nine years old.

•CHAPTER ONE•
THE PRIMARIES★

Good morning, Kitty!

Kitty? Kitty?

Wow. Something outside really has your attention today. I wonder what it is. Are there birds? Are there squirrels? Did Brian the mailman drop his lunch again?

Oh, I see. You're looking at some of those stray cats that come wandering in from the neighborhood next to ours every now and then.

What's the big deal, Kitty? They're not hurting anyone, are they? They're just cats like you.

Well, Kitty, if they're bothering you so much, why don't you do something about it?

I know that look, Kitty. You're thinking about throwing them all into an active volcano, aren't you? *Sigh* That's not what I was talking about.

What I mean is . . . why don't you run for president of the Neighborhood Cat Club? Old Kitty is about to leave office, which means that a new president has to be elected. It might as well be you.

Oh, sure . . . I know that being president is a great responsibility and a lot of hard work. And I know that it requires a lot of personal sacrifice. But maybe you'd do a great job.

And besides, it's the best way I can think of to deal with the stray cat issue in the way that you want most.

That's right, Kitty. As president, you would get to suggest the laws that all of the other kitties would have to follow, including any law you think would be best for dealing with the stray cats . . . with the possible exception of throwing them all into an active volcano.

You see, Kitty, as president you would . . . uh . . .

Where'd she go?

Sorry, Kitty. It's just not that simple. You have to go through a whole lot of very complicated steps before you can become president.

That's just how it is, Kitty. Elections★ might seem complicated, but that's what keeps them fair.

Why, even BEFORE you get elected to be president, you have to win ANOTHER election just so you can have the honor of running for president in the first place.

This first election is called a primary, and wouldn't you know it—today happens to be primary day! That's why all of the other kitties from the neighborhood are here. Hello, kitties!

Now, all we need to do is figure out how to hold a primary election. And who better to ask than good ol' UNCLE MURRAY.

MEOW MEOW *

* Hi! Sorry we're late, but we thought you said "library" instead of "primary" and we got caught up reading *Harry Paw-ter*. Ha-ha! Get it?

25

UNCLE MURRAY'S FUN FACTS

WHAT ARE PRIMARIES?

What . . no cat questions?

Okey-dokey! Questions about politics! Now THIS is something I know about. Let me just put on my special election day hat!

So, what is a primary, Uncle Murray?

Well, in a primary you vote for a candidate to become a nominee.★

Huh?

It's easy. See, most elections have at least two political groups that want to be in charge, and these groups are called parties.★ But before you have an election, each group has to nominate someone they want to represent them, so they hold a primary. How do you pick the right nominee? You hold a primary.

Great. So how do we hold a primary?

Well, first you gotta pick your delegates.★

26

The what?

Delegates. Delegates are the people who represent your party's nominee. So, first you pick your delegates, and then you vote for your nominee, and then the person who gets the most votes gets the most delegates who will then represent him or her at the convention.★

Convention?

Oh, yeah! Those are fun. That's where all the delegates get together and choose their nominee for the election.

So, in other words, a nominee is chosen at a convention by a bunch of delegates who go there to represent the candidate chosen at a primary . . .

Or caucus!★

Caucus?!!

Caucuses are awesome! Instead of primaries, some states have caucuses, which are like big meetings in which a bunch of people try to convince each other of who would be the best nominee by standing on tables and waving flags and shouting a lot.

AAAAARGH!

Yeah, like that.

That was just way, way, WAY too confusing.

Since you all look about as bewildered as I do, kitties, let's try something else.

No one knows why, but for some reason, anyone who campaigns for any political office has to be good at kissing babies. So let's have a contest—let's pick our nominees by seeing which kitties are best at kissing Baby!

I know you're enjoying your french fries, Baby, but we need you!

* I smell potatoes, salt, and grease!

The kitties are split into two parties—the kitties who live on the LEFT side of the street and the kitties who live on the RIGHT side of the street. First, it's the Left Side Party's turn to kiss the baby.

Chatty Kitty, do you want to kiss the baby?

MEOW MEOW MEOW

MEOW
MEOW
MEOW
MEOW MEOW
MEOW*

MEOW
MEOW
MEOW

NOIZ!

Never mind.

Do you want to try, Big Kitty?

SLURP!

GIGGLE!

Big Kitty wins the primary for the Left Side of the Street Party! It probably didn't hurt that Baby was eating french fries.

* If we didn't have lips, then we'd have to kiss with our ears, which would be funny because then we wouldn't see who we were kissing, but we could hear each other's thoughts. If we didn't have noses, then we'd have to kiss with our noses, and if we didn't have noses, then we'd have to kiss with our noses, and if we didn't have noses, then we'd have to kiss with our noses, and if we didn't have each other's thoughts.

And now it's time for the kitties from the Right Side of the Street to kiss Baby. You're first, Pretty Kitty, and Stinky Kitty is next.

Well, Kitty, now's your big chance. If you manage to kiss Baby you will win the Right Side of the Street primary and be their nominee for the election. All you have to do is . . .

KISS BABY.
KISS BABY.
KISS BABY.
KISS BABY.
ISS BA

YOU DID IT, KITTY! That means you won the primary and that you and Big Kitty are the two nominees who will run against each other to become president!

Thank you, Baby.

•CHAPTER TWO•
THE ENDORSEMENT★

Well, Kitty . . . Now's the hard part. Now you have to find ways to convince enough kitties that you would be the best candidate to vote for on election day. This long, hard process of convincing voters that you deserve their vote is known as a campaign.★

We don't have much money to spend, Kitty, so one thing we can do is conduct a grassroots campaign.★ Do you know what that is, Kitty? That's when we dig hard to find the roots of what voters care about and then try to leave something of ourselves behind for them to ponder.

JUMPIN' JEHOSAPHAT! NO, KITTY, NO!

THAT'S NOT WHAT I MEANT!

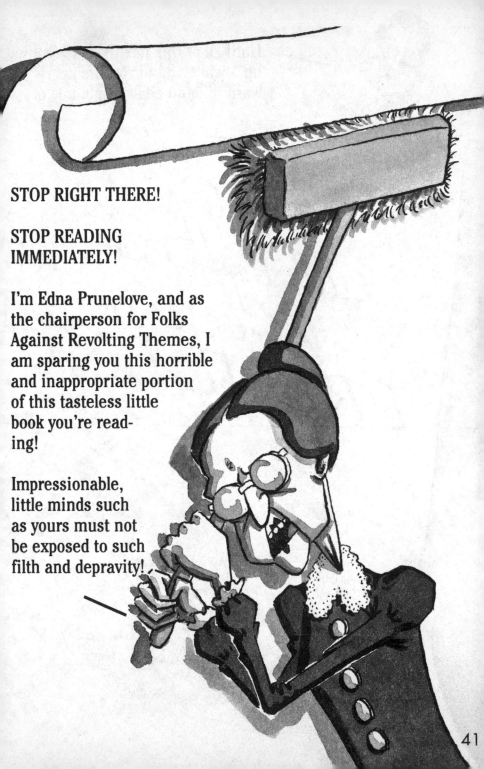

STOP RIGHT THERE!

STOP READING
IMMEDIATELY!

I'm Edna Prunelove, and as
the chairperson for Folks
Against Revolting Themes, I
am sparing you this horrible
and inappropriate portion
of this tasteless little
book you're read-
ing!

Impressionable,
little minds such
as yours must not
be exposed to such
filth and depravity!

41

Once upon a time, there was a happy little puppy who wanted to be president of the United States.

"Wouldn't it be grand," he thought, "to be the president? Then I could make sure all the children had bones to chew on, and squeaky rubbery toys to play with, and tasty pigs' ears to eat whenever they wanted!"

So, the happy little puppy traveled far and wide, from state to state in his campaign, asking all the good people in the country to vote for him.

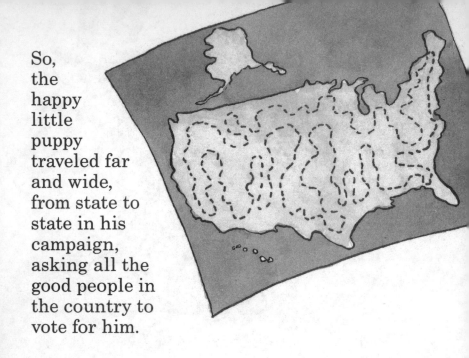

All of the people he met were so pleased to meet such a happy little puppy.

"Of course we'll vote for such a happy little puppy!" they all said.

"Woof!" said the puppy happily. And all of the people laughed.

But then on election day, just as all of the good people were about to vote, they suddenly realized . . .

"Wait a minute! He's not a native-born citizen!★ He's not over thirty-five years old! He hasn't lived in the United States for at least fourteen years!

"He's just a stupid dog! What the heck are we doing here?!"

So, the happy little puppy wasn't elected president of the United States, after all.

The End

There, now. Wasn't that just lovely? Such warmth! Such humor! And I think we all learned something. I can't wait for the movie!

And now back to your nasty little book about that nasty little cat.

Wow, Kitty! Those people sure were upset about their lawn. NEVER do that again!

Kitty, a grassroots campaign is the kind of campaign in which you try to communicate directly with your voters by going door-to-door, working locally, and trying to make personal contact with voters any way you can.

It's not . . . uh . . . that thing you did.

A grassroots campaign is the kind of campaign you can conduct when you just don't have a lot of money like us. So, one of the things we can do without any money is get Old Kitty's endorsement. If Old Kitty is willing to publicly recommend you for the office of president, then all of those kitties who once voted for him might vote for YOU this time.

SNORE

And it looks like Big Kitty had the same idea!

I guess this means that Old Kitty is just going to have to make a choice . . .

as soon as he wakes up.

Which might take . . .

a . . .

little . . .

while.

51

Oh, well. I don't think either of you will be getting an endorsement today.

Maybe it's time to look at other options, Kitty.

•CHAPTER THREE•

ON THE CAMPAIGN TRAIL

Okay, Kitty . . . let's try something else. Another common part of conducting a grassroots campaign is simply going door-to-door to meet as many voters as you can. This way, you get to know which issues your voters care most about. And they get to hear how you plan to address their issues.

Doesn't that sound like fun?

Let's try this house, Kitty.

You need to make a good first impression, Kitty. Try to greet the voters with a nice smile.

Can you smile, Kitty?

On second thought, forget the smile, Kitty. I'll just ring the doorbell.

Look, Kitty! It's your good friend Chatty Kitty! I'm sure she has lots of important things to say. Let's find out what . . .

* Hi. Running for president? Great! Did you know that Abraham Lincoln was the first president of the United States to own a cat in the White House? His name was Tabby. But more importantly, the nineteenth president, Rutherford Hayes, owned the very first Siamese cat, named Siam, ever to live in the United States. It's possible that I'm related to her, even though I've never been to the White House. I once saw a house that was white, but I don't think it was the same place.

And Theodore Roosevelt owned two cats named Slippers and Tom Quartz. And Calvin Coolidge owned four cats named Smokey, Blackie, Timmy, and Tiger, which might sound like a lot of cats, but he also kept twelve dogs, two raccoons, and a pygmy hippo, so go figure.

Woodrow Wilson had a cat named Puffins. John F. Kennedy owned a cat named Tom Kitten. Gerald Ford owned a cat named Shan. And Jimmy Carter's daughter, Amy, owned a cat (another Siamese!) named Misty Malarky Ying Yang, which is very hard to say ten times fast, but I can try . . . Misty Malarky Ying Yang, Misty Malarky Ying Yang, Misty . . .

MEOW MEOW MEOW MEOW MEOW MEOW MEOW MEOW MEOW MEOW MEOW*

=GASP=

Quick, Kitty! Chatty Kitty is finally taking a breath! Now's your chance to tell her why you would be the best candidate to vote for!

Ronald Reagan had two cats named Cleo and Sara. Bill Clinton had a cat named Socks. And George W. Bush had a cat named India.

A FISH?!

NO, KITTY! You can't give Chatty Kitty a fish to convince her to vote for you! That's known as "buying a vote" and it's illegal!

*Did you know that there's a species of mullet known as the "President's Fish"? It's also known as the "Ludong" or the "Banali," and it's close to extinction because of overfishing in the Philippines.

60

Get rid of the fish, and let's go to the next house. You should know better than that, Kitty.

I'll ring the doorbell here.

Look, Kitty! Your opponent Big Kitty lives here! Isn't that a coincidence! Hi, Big Kitty!

Now, Kitty. That is no way to behave even toward your opponent. Besides, what would happen if someone had a . . .

. . . camera.

Uh-oh.

•CHAPTER FOUR•

MEDIA AND MONEY

Good morning, Kitty. Are you ready for another day of pounding the pavement and knocking on doors for your campaign?

Oh! What's this, Kitty? Today's newspaper?

DAILY NOOZ

HISSY-FIT

CAT CANDIDATE FREAKS OUT

Neighbors up and down the block awoke yesterday to a truly horrible, frightening, sheiking noise. That noise, as it turns out, was Kitty, the ___ of the Block nominee for ___ borhood Cat ___

"I didn't kr
noise was.
"I though'
a steamr
over a d
maybe
a rake
board
Chrys

Polic
the

68

Well, I wouldn't worry too much about this, Kitty. People will forget all about this soon enough. And once we begin discussing the issues they care most about, I think we can rely on the voters to make an educated decision.

It's just a good thing there wasn't a video camera there to record . . .

Hmmm . . . Well, I guess that Big Kitty is a pretty shrewd campaigner after all.

But never mind all that, Kitty. Let's go out and pound the pavement! Let's go knock on some . . .

No? Why aren't you coming with me, Kitty?

Kitty? What are you trying to tell me?

Are . . . are . . . are you FIRING me, Kitty?

Are you serious?

Wow. I really didn't see that coming.

But how will you run your campaign without me? You need me, don't you?

Don't you?

74

You have your own campaign Web site? But how? You couldn't have done this yourself. And who would be goofy enough to make a campaign Web site for a CAT? Who would be so irresponsible as to make a campaign Web site for YOU? Who could you have possibly tricked into . . .

Oh.

Am I
troub

UNCLE MURRAY'S FUN FACTS

WHY DID YOU DO IT?!

Hey, don't yell at me! The cat offered me a pretty good-looking fish, and I was hungry. Besides, a political campaign can cost a lot of money.

How much money?

Well, in the United States, some presidential campaigns can cost more than a billion dollars!

A BILLION DOLLARS! HOLY %#@$.

I know. Candidates have been known to spend more than a hundred million dollars just to run for mayor!

So, where do they get all that money?

Well, some of these guys are pretty rich to begin with, so they use some of their own money. But most of them get donations from people or groups that really want to see them get elected.

What kinds of people?

All kinds of people. You don't have to be rich to donate. People can donate

76

just a couple of bucks. But you can't donate more than $2,700 to a candidate. That's supposed to keep really rich people from controlling an election.

Okay, then what kinds of groups?

Well, some are called PACs or Political Action Committees.* Those are organizations that have a specific agenda and want to get candidates elected to help them. They can donate as much as $5,000 to a candidate during the primary and again during the final election—totaling $10,000, but no more.

What do candidates do with all that money?

Well, they need it for traveling and buying ads and commercials for TV. Although not all of those ads come from the candidates.

Who else is there?

There are these so-called Super PACs* that can collect and spend as much money as they want, sometimes even millions and millions and millions of dollars. They buy ads and commercials and can say anything they want—so long as they don't work with or for a candidate.

Smells kind of fishy to me.

Ooh! Sorry, my fish must be done. Want some?

77

First of all, Kitty, I can't believe there are people out there who are goofy enough to send you money. But I suppose if Uncle Murray was goofy enough to make you a Web site so you can find people goofy enough to send you money, then I suppose anything is possible.

So, what do you plan to do with your money anyway?

Why are you picking up that remote, Kitty? Is it time for *Paw and Order* or *All My Kittens* or . . .

No. You didn't. Please tell me you didn't.

You did.

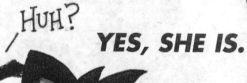

Well, Kitty . . . That commercial may be the most revolting thing I've ever seen on television.

Kitty, you can't just make yourself out to be what you think people want to see. If you want to be president, then you HAVE to be honest about who you are.

Plus, voters care about issues. You have to tell voters where you stand on the things they care about most. Have you forgotten all about the stray cat issue? That's why you were running for president in the first place.

Now, please tell me that you have something more to show that will address the important issues of the day.

HEH HEH HEH

CLICK

What do we really know about Big Kitty?

Oh, sure. He's big. But lots of things are big.

Elephants are big.

Cars are big.

And dogs are big.

That's right.

DOGS.

Big, stupid, sloppy dogs that stink and drool and poop wherever the heck they want.

Big Kitty is as big as a dog.

It makes you wonder . . .

Could Big Kitty really BE a DOG?

Paid for by the Coalition to Make Sure That Dogs Are Not Secretly Elected to Be President of the Neighborhood Cat Club

"The Coalition to Make Sure That Dogs Are Not Secretly Elected to be President of the Neighborhood Cat Club"?! What the %#@$ is that?

Oh, Kitty, you went and found some Super PAC that would go out there and smear poor Big Kitty just to further your campaign, didn't you? You know that Big Kitty isn't really a dog, don't you?

Don't give me that big, innocent look, Kitty! I don't care that you're not the one who actually made the ad, and I don't care that you're not even mentioned in the ad.

You claim to know nothing about the organization that made this ad, but I don't believe it for a second.

Hello? Yes?

I see.

Okay. I'll tell her. Thank you.

Goodbye.

Well, Kitty . . . Now you'll have to put your money where your mouth is. You've been invited to have a public debate★ with Big Kitty on the day before the election.

That's right. Now you'll have to stand before all the voters and explain to them just why you should be their best choice to represent them as their president.

Kitty?

Kitty?

Uh-oh.

•CHAPTER FIVE•
THE DEBATE

Good evening, and welcome to the one and only debate between the two nominees hoping to earn your vote in tomorrow's election for president of the Neighborhood Cat Club.

I'm Strange Kitty, your moderator★ for tonight's debate.

I will ask each candidate a question about an issue that is important to the voters from both sides of the street. Each candidate will have one minute to respond after which both candidates will each have thirty seconds to give a rebuttal, or an opposing viewpoint.

We'll begin with a coin toss to see who goes first.

Hang on! I'll try to find something else!

Live television, folks.

I found something!

Cool! What is it?

It's my *Power Panther* Fan Club Medallion!

Awesome! Where did you get it?

They were giving them out at last week's San Francisco *Power Panther* Science Fiction and Comic Book Convention.

Oh . . . right.

HARUMPF!

HUFF PUFF

What was I thinking? I have them all recorded anyway.

You do?

I've never seen the one where AquaCat is hypnotized by Pirate Puma and eats melon!

That's a good one. Wanna come over to watch it?

You bet!

Great! Let's go to my place right after the . . . um . . . oh, right! The debate!

Let's just start with you, Big Kitty . . .

Where do you stand on the issue of stray cats who wander in from other neighborhoods to live on our street? Do we welcome them and let them live here or do we chase them away? Please keep your response to one minute . . . starting NOW!

You "like french fries."

Is that really all you have to say?

You "REALLY like french fries." I understand. But the stray cat question is a pretty big issue, isn't it? I mean, we sometimes get these stray cats wandering into our neighborhood who want to live here. We live in nice, warm houses with toys and litter boxes and cool stuff like *Power Panther* medallions. Should we be expected to share our stuff with these cats who have nothing—nothing at all? Or should we take steps to keep these cats out because we don't know who they are?

MEOW?

 No, I don't have any french fries.

sigh

The same question goes to you, Kitty. Where do you stand on the stray cats issue? Do we . . .

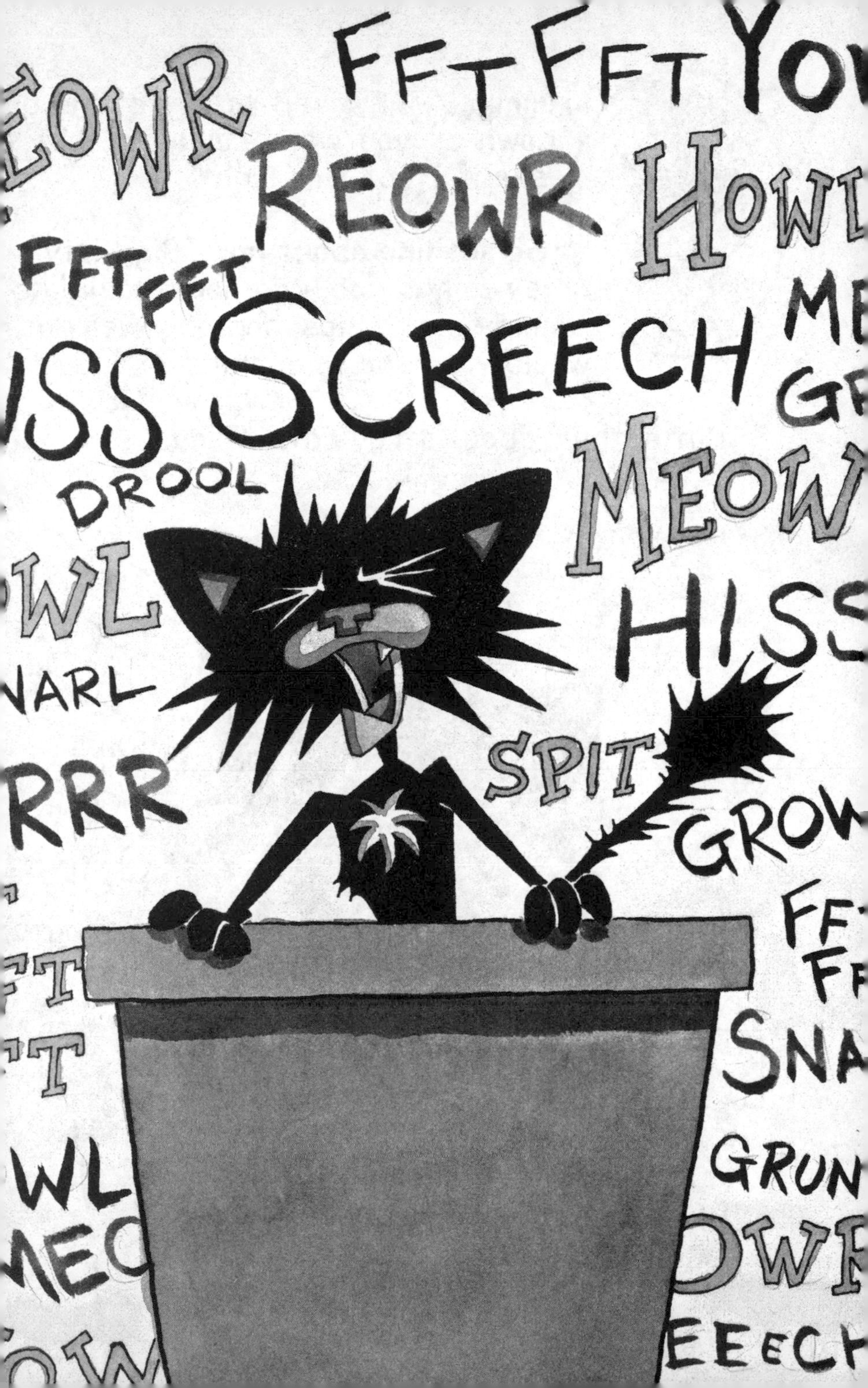
FFT FFT
REOWR
FFT FFT
SCREECH
DROOL
SPIT

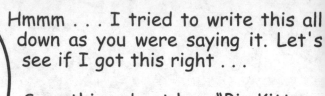

Hmmm . . . I tried to write this all down as you were saying it. Let's see if I got this right . . .

Something about how "Big Kitty is really a dog, and dogs smell like moldy corn chips, and only weirdos would vote for corn chips."

But nothing about stray cats. Okay.

HUFF
PUFF
HUFF
PUFF
HUFF
PUFF

105

•CHAPTER SIX•

ELECTION DAY!

Well, Kitty . . . The big day is finally here. The only thing you have to do now is actually vote here at this polling station.★

Let's take a look at what the ballot★ looks like.

Oh, sure. There's always a "WRITE-IN"★ option. This gives the voter the chance to vote for anyone he or she wants if the official candidates aren't deemed worthy. Voting is all about choosing, Kitty. And it's always good to have more options . . . right?

Anyway, it's your turn to vote, Kitty.

Hello, Strange Kitty. Nice job last night.

Kitty is here to cast her ballot.

Kitty! Are you telling me that you never registered to vote? You HAVE to register to vote! Registering is one of the most important responsibilities of being a citizen!

UNCLE MURRAY'S FUN FACTS

WHAT IS VOTER REGISTRATION?

Voter registration is a process of collecting all of the names and addresses of everyone who can vote.

But why do you need to register?

Well, the main reason is to prevent voter fraud. The law is that you can only vote once, and you can only vote in the area where you live. Registering to vote creates a database that ensures that you only vote one time in the place where you live, and it makes sure you're even allowed to vote.

Really? Are some people not allowed to vote?

Oh, sure! For one thing, you have to be over eighteen years old. Sorry, kids. Also, in the United States you have to be a citizen of the country. Plus, depending on the state, if you commit a felony, a bad crime, you may not be allowed to vote at all, even after you get out of prison.

Okay, so how do you register?

It couldn't be easier. All you gotta do is fill out a voter registration form. They're super easy to find. You can download them from the Internet. You can go to your local board of elections. Usually, you can just go to your local library or post office and see if they have any hanging around.

When do you register?

In most states, you have to register to vote as much as a month before an election. There are a few states like Maine and Wisconsin that let you register on the same day you vote, but it's best to play it safe and register WAY ahead of time . . . unless you live in North Dakota where you don't have to register at all. I'm not sure why—that's just how they do things in the Peace Garden State.

If kids can't vote, is there anything we can do for an election?

Absolutely! What you do is go home, find a grown-up, and say, "Hey, you! Did you register?" And if they say, "Not yet," then you have them read what your ol' Uncle Murray has to say about it. Then on election day you go, "Hey, you! Did you vote?" And if they say, "Not yet," then you keep asking over and over again until they do it. It's that important!

KITTY! This means that you can't vote! You can't even vote for yourself! This is a disaster!

Let's just hope that enough of the other kitties vote for you.

•CHAPTER SEVEN•
THE RESULTS

Well, I guess I should have seen this . . .

One vote for Big Kitty . . .
One vote for Pretty Kitty . . .
One vote for Stinky Kitty . . .

* Misty Malarky Ying Yang, Misty Malarky Ying Yang, Misty Malarky . . .

Being cats, and being just a little self-centered, all of the kitties voted for themselves—except for the Twin Kitties who voted for each other.

You, too?

Yup. Do you blame me?

KITTY - 0
BIG KITTY - 1
PRETTY KITTY - 1
STINKY KITTY - 1
TWIN KITTY #1 - 1
TWIN KITTY #2 - 1
CHATTY KITTY - 1
STRANGE KITTY - 1

Well, Kitty . . . You may have lost the election, but none of the other kitties actually won. They're all tied at ONE VOTE each!

This is pretty serious, Kitty. Without a clear winner, you kitties won't have a president!

This means that unless something very dramatic happens, there will probably have to be another election. You might still have a chance after all, Kitty.

HMMM...

DING DONG!

Hold that thought, Kitty. There's the doorbell.

Now, this is interesting. It's a letter from Old Kitty.

And not just any letter! It's an absentee ballot!★

OLD KITTY
NEIGHBORHOOD POLLING PLACE
10591

Kitty, absentee ballots are for voters who can't make it to the polling place on election day for whatever reason. Sometimes it's because the voter knows he'll be out of town or because he's physically unable to go to the polls—like Old Kitty.

Let's open the envelope and find out how Old Kitty voted! This is a pretty dramatic moment, isn't it, Kitty? I wish we had some music.

It's one more vote for Strange Kitty!

This means that Strange Kitty won the election and is the next president of the Neighborhood Cat Club!

Well, Kitty . . . That settles it. S.K. won the election and will be the next president. I'm sorry you didn't win, Kitty. I'm sorry you didn't even get the chance to vote. I'm sorry no one else voted for you.

I know you tried hard to win the election, Kitty. But I hope you learned an important lesson today about how to run a clean campaign and . . .

Kitty?

Kitty?

Uh-oh.

NO, KITTY! NOT THIS TIME!

You don't get to throw one of your screaming, spitting, angry, crazy hissy fits this time! You don't get to be a BAD KITTY this time!

I don't care if you're upset, Kitty! I don't even care that you lost. Elections are about more than who runs for office. Elections are about more than who wins and who loses. Elections are about more than campaigns and TV commercials and money.

Oh, I can't do that! The kitties need to decide how good a job I'm doing for themselves!

Elections are all about **DEMOCRACY!**★

We saw democracy in action today, Kitty, when we watched Strange Kitty win the election fair and square. Because that's what democracy does. Democracy makes sure that EVERYONE has a chance to participate, that EVERYONE has a chance to win, and that EVERYONE has the chance to someday become the leader of his or her community.

See? That's how I know you'll be a great president.

You may not like how the election ended, Kitty. But you have no choice but to live with the results if you want to live in a democracy.

135

•APPENDIX ONE•

EDNA'S LOVELY LITTLE GLOSSARY OF ELECTION TERMS

Hello, Children! Edna Prunelove here. And now that you've suffered all the way through that sordid little story about that rude little cat and her gross little adventures, I thought I would reward you with something educational. I thought it would be grand to review all of those complicated little words you saw about the election. Won't this be amusing? Let's review them in the order in which they appear.

PRESIDENT • Well, this is as good a place to start as any. What is a "president"? Essentially, a president is the man or woman who has been selected by a group of people to

be in charge of that group of people. It doesn't matter how big that group is. Not just countries have presidents. Some companies have presidents. Even some classrooms have presidents. Perhaps this will inspire you to run for president in your classroom. What fun!

OFFICE • In terms of a presidency, "office" is used the same way as "power." A president who is "in office" is "in power," which means that he or she's in charge. Likewise, if the president is "out of office" or not president anymore, then he's "out of power." Bye-bye!

PRIMARY • Now it starts to get complicated. Before you can have a president, you have to figure out WHO is going to run for president. One way is to hold a primary, which is a lot like an . . .

ELECTION • . . . but not quite. An election is a process in which someone is chosen to be in office. But a primary is like an election BEFORE the election in which you choose who will run in the election. Confused yet? You're not alone. There are people who dedicate their whole lives to studying how elections work.

NOMINEE • Everyone who runs in a primary is a "candidate." Whoever wins the primary becomes the nominee who can now run in the election. The nominee was chosen by the people in his or her party.

PARTY • OH, JOY! IT'S A PARTY! Where are the balloons? The music? Cake? Ice cream? I'm just having a little fun with you. It's not that kind of party. In this case, we're talking about a political party, which is a group of people who all have the same philosophy and goal of getting their nominee to win the election.

DELEGATES • Because a person running for office can't be everywhere at the same time, that person has to have delegates who go around representing him or her. If you think of nominees as being like rock-and-roll stars, then their delegates are like those silly little fans who run around trying to convince everyone to love their nominee as much as they do. (We all know people like that.) To make things even more complicated, often delegates are themselves ELECTED.

CONVENTION • OH, JOY! IT'S A PARTY! I mean it this time! This time there really are balloons and music and cake and very colorful (which is a nice way of saying "ugly") shirts and yelling and screaming. Why? Because everyone in the political party has finally gotten together at a convention and chosen a nominee to run in the election.

CAUCUS • Instead of having all the zany fun of a primary, some states choose to have the zany fun of a caucus, which is less like an election and more like a big meeting of people in the party who get together to choose a nominee. So, instead of having people come in one at a time to vote everybody shows up all at once and decides together in a caucus.

ENDORSEMENT • Maybe it's because politicians are just naturally insecure people, but they all really love endorsements. An endorsement is when someone gives a nominee a public statement of approval or support. This statement can be very useful to a nominee.

CAMPAIGN • When you conduct a bunch of activities, all of them coordinated for a specific purpose like getting a nominee elected, that's called a campaign. In the United States, a campaign can last for years and cost a LOT of money.

GRASSROOTS CAMPAIGN • The roots of grass are just below the surface of the ground. So the idea of a grassroots campaign is to try and find out what affects the people who will vote for you. The best way to do this, of course, is to simply go out and talk to as many people as you can. And that's exactly what a lot of nominees do.

NATIVE-BORN CITIZEN • There are only three conditions necessary to being the president of the United States. You have to be over thirty-five years old, you have to have lived in the United States for at least fourteen years, and you have to have been born somewhere inside the United States—but if both of your parents are U.S. citizens, then you can be born anywhere in the world, even the North Pole! That would be exciting.

PAC • No, I'm not talking about that irritating little video game with that thing that eats the dots. Political Action Committees, or PACs, are organizations that collect and spend money in order to influence an election. They can donate money to the candidates themselves, but then they can only donate $10,000 at most. And sometimes they buy advertisements, on which they can spend as much money as they want.

Super PAC • A super PAC is a PAC without limits. It can collect and spend as much money as it wants. The money they collect can come from almost anywhere, sometimes even from organizations that hide the names of its members, which means that no one will ever know who gave them the money. But super PACs are not allowed to donate any money directly to a candidate or to coordinate with them at all. They have to support a candidate or oppose a candidate with their massive truck loads of money all on their own.

DEBATE • When two or more people get together to publically argue over one or many topics, this is called a debate.

MODERATOR • This is the person who runs the debate. He or she asks the questions, controls the amount of time each person has to speak, and in general tries to keep the event as fair as possible. Think of a moderator as being like the referee in a boxing match, but with fewer punches being thrown.

POLLING STATION • Quite simply, this is the place where you go to vote.

BALLOT • This is a device, and it can simply be a piece of paper, that records your vote. It's called a *ballot* because a long time ago, people often voted by putting little balls into a box. A white ball meant "yes" and a black ball meant "no." Isn't that interesting? Yes, I think so, too.

WRITE-IN CANDIDATE • If a nominee's name does not appear on the ballot, you still have the option to write the nominee's name down as your vote. Why, the nominee doesn't even have to be running for the office. This might sound silly, but many nominees have won office this way. Isn't that nice?

REGISTER • But before you vote, you have to register. I think that funny little man Uncle Murray explained it quite nicely. You can go back to page 112 if you need to be reminded.

ABSENTEE BALLOT • These are special ballots for people who are simply unable to make their way to the polling place on election day. In most states you do not have to give an excuse as to why you have to use an absentee ballot. But you should be careful. Send it at least a week in advance of election day, because most absentee ballots are mailed in. Apparently, the postal system is quite efficient in that rude little cat's neighborhood.

DEMOCRACY • Ah, democracy. One of my favorite words in the world. I like it even more than "gladiola" and "lagoon." A wise man named Abraham Lincoln once essentially described democracy as government of the people, by the people, and for the people. The key word here, of course, is "people." A democracy is not a government run by a king who never gives up his throne. A democracy is not a government run by a dictator who never gives up his office. A democracy is a government run by people and where elections decide everything. Elections certainly are complicated, but I hope you understand now just how *sniff* important they are.

sniff Forgive me if I get a little teary-eyed. I am rather prone to emotional outbursts of patriotism sometimes. I'm sure you're the same way.

sniff, sniff Oh, dear! It appears my sensibilities really have gotten the better of me. I must go compose myself. I do hope you all learned something today. Ta-Ta!

•APPENDIX TWO•

During any dramatic moments in this book, please play the following music on your tuba, zither, or harpsichord.

Thank you.

Arrangement by Heike Doerr

Dear Nick Bruel,

Thank you for finishing these sentences.

XO,

SQUARE
FISH

Old Kitty will . . .

Old Kitty will retire now that he's fulfilled his second term in office. There is a long tradition among retired presidents that they open special libraries that commemorate their terms in office, and Old Kitty is no different. He will open The Old Kitty Neighborhood Library, which will chronicle his many achievements while in office as well as that unfortunate scandal in which his administration was caught trading catnip for shiny laser toys.

The hardest part about being president is . . .

The hardest part about being president, I imagine, is knowing that no matter what you do or say, there will always be someone who strongly disagrees with whatever you do and whatever you say. Recognizing that you can never please all of the people all of the time is one thing, but recognizing that your every action and your every word are guaranteed to anger someone somewhere must be difficult.

Kitty laws are . . .

Kitty laws are not designed to benefit dogs or fish or mice or gorillas or porcupines or macaroni penguins or any other animal not fortunate enough to be a cat. Personally, I'm not sure I would want to live in a world where its rules are dictated exclusively by cats.

Elections are . . .

Elections are precious. There are currently 47 countries in the world in which there is no voting process at all. And then there are many, many countries in which the voting process is so corrupt and crooked that elections are decided long before a single vote is cast. So, when a voter happens to live in a country with a free and functional democracy, then there is no reason for that voter to not participate in the election.

Political parties can be . . .

Political parties can be liquid. If you do your research and look at the values and issues any political party cared about 100 years, 50 years, or even 20 years ago, you'll find that they can be very different from what they hold dear today.

Kissing babies . . .

Kissing babies is a sometimes unsanitary tradition candidates often go through while running for president. The babies themselves rarely come out of it with positive memories.

Edna Prunelove loves . . .

Edna Prunelove loves democracy. She just can't get enough of it. She eats democracy pancakes for breakfast. She eats democracy sandwiches for lunch. She swims in democracy swimming pools for exercise and wears her democracy dancing shoes when she dances her democracy dance. To the casual observer, Edna Prunelove might seem a little one-sided in her passion, but her passion happens to have many facets.

If the happy little puppy had been elected President of the United States . . .

If the happy little puppy had been elected as President of the United States, we would live in a country where squeaky chew toys are currency, taxes could be paid with pig ears, and poop scoop laws would no longer be enforced.

Big Kitty's campaign . . .

Big Kitty's campaign was doomed from the start. He was passive. He showed no enthusiasm in his efforts to win. He remained unfocused on his opponent. And he seemed uninterested in the important issues of the day. Big Kitty might have meant well, but his lack of passion gave very little incentive to voters.

Kitty's campaign . . .

Kitty's campaign was doomed from the start. She was excessively aggressive. She revealed that she was not above underhanded tactics to win the election. She often focused less on the election than on attacking her opponent. And she seemed uninterested in the important issues of the day. Ultimately, she made herself unrelatable to voters. Is it any wonder that voters turned to an alternative candidate?

If Kitty had a running mate . . .

If Kitty had a running mate, it probably wouldn't be another cat. Kitty doesn't have a strong history of working well with other cats. Her running mate would probably not be Mouse, since appetizers rarely make good running mates. And it certainly wouldn't be a dog. Possibly, Kitty's best running mate might be a mirror she carried and held up while campaigning, but this still wouldn't guarantee that she won't sometimes angrily quarrel with her own reflection.

If I were president . . .

If I were president, I would invest more in education. I have a pretty simple theory . . . if you want to see a future with a smart, happy planet, then it has to be populated by smart, happy people. Smart, happy people can only come from smart, happy schools. And, like it or not, smart, happy schools need the resources that can only come from money and funding.

Bad Kitty for President

Host Your Own Mock Election!

Curious how the Neighborhood Cat Coalition keeps their checks and balances?

Host your own mock election at school or home today. Here's all the stuff you'll need for a smooth-sailing election. Just don't let Bad Kitty into the ballot box!

Official Petitions

Have a school or community official encourage students to participate in the election by signing up as candidates for specific positions.

Campaign Speeches

Whether you are running for class president or student council member, it is always a great idea to hold an assembly where all of the candidates talk about their platforms and ideas. They should discuss issues that might have an effect on the student experience.

Election Ballot

Have everyone who is interested in the election cast their vote individually and privately. Create a box with a small slit for the ballots. The ballots could look like this:

I give my vote to:

My Write-In Candidate is:

Tallying Ballots

Once the voting has closed, assign a group of students to count all of the votes. Use a chalkboard, a white board, or even a computer chart to make sure every vote is counted, and every voice is heard. Once all of the votes have been counted, you can announce the winner!

Bad Kitty for President
Where Is Bad Kitty Campaigning?

Help! We've got to find Kitty's campaign trail! Use the clues to locate the states Kitty has visited, and where she will be going to next.

Put a paw print (and a number) on the states where you find Kitty!

Clues:

1. This Midwestern state is known for its cheese and cooooooold winters. Go Packers, Go!
2. This state is known for its aloha spirit and delicious pineapples! Aloha!
3. This state is known for its loyal sports fans and historic Freedom Trail. It's the Bay State!
4. This "sunny" state is known for its yummy oranges, fun theme parks, and boggy Everglades.
5. This state shares a border with Canada and is part of the Great Plains region. It is located just north of another state with a similar name!
6. This Northeast state is home to the busiest, most populated city in the U.S.—the state and the city have the same name!
7. This Pacific state is known for the historic Gold Rush. It is also home to Tinseltown and some of the best surfing!
8. Commonly known as the Lone Star State, it is home to the Alamo!
9. Located in the west, this state is home to some of the best skiing and hiking trails in our country. It's home to the Rocky Mountains!
10. This Northwest state is the only state to be named after a president.

Bad Kitty for President
Writing Exercise!

Every candidate needs a good writing team! Become a part of Bad Kitty's campaign by helping her write a speech to read at the next Neighborhood Cat Coalition.

On a piece of paper, make a box like the one below and outline your ideas. Then, on a separate sheet, use these points to write your final speech. And remember, no empty promises, Kitty!

Introduction:

Main Argument:

Conclusion:

It's time for this sick kitty to go to the vet!

Keep reading for a sneak peek of
Bad Kitty Goes to the Vet.

CHAPTER ONE

POOR, SICK KITTY

This is what Kitty looks like when she's a happy, healthy pussycat.

She has lots of energy.

She has a good appetite.

And she keeps herself nice and clean.

But that's not how Kitty looks today. She looks terrible. She looks tired. She looks unhappy. She does not look healthy at all.

And worst of all . . . Kitty is just not eating her food.